GOSCINNY AND UDERZO
PRESENT
An Asterix Adventure

ASTERIX
IN
BRITAIN

Written by RENÉ GOSCINNY *and Illustrated by* ALBERT UDERZO

Translated by Anthea Bell *and* Derek Hockridge

Asterix titles available now

Coming soon

© 1966 GOSCINNY/UDERZO

Revised edition and English translation © 2005 HACHETTE
Original title: *Astérix chez les Bretons*

Exclusive licensee: Orion Publishing Group
Translators: Anthea Bell and Derek Hockridge
Typography: Bryony Newhouse

This revised edition first published in Great Britain by Orion Publishing Group

This paperback edition first published in 2005 by Orion Books Ltd,
Orion House, 5 Upper Saint Martin's Lane, London WC2H 9EA

3 5 7 9 10 8 6 4 2

Printed in France by Partenaires

http://gb.asterix.com
www.orionbooks.co.uk

A CIP record for this book is available from the British Library

ISBN 0 75286 618 4 (cased)
ISBN 0 75286 619 2 (paperback)

Distributed in the United States of America by Sterling Publishing Co. Inc.
387 Park Avenue South, New York, NY 10016

GAULISH VILLAGE

COMPENDIUM

LAUDANUM

AQUARIUM

TOTORUM

ARMORICA

BELGICA

• LUTETIA

SPQR

GAUL
(ROMAN CONQUEST)
50 BC

CELTICA

AQUITANIA

PROVINCIA

THE YEAR IS 50 BC. GAUL IS ENTIRELY OCCUPIED BY THE
ROMANS. WELL, NOT ENTIRELY ... ONE SMALL VILLAGE OF
INDOMITABLE GAULS STILL HOLDS OUT AGAINST THE INVADERS.
AND LIFE IS NOT EASY FOR THE ROMAN LEGIONARIES WHO
GARRISON THE FORTIFIED CAMPS OF TOTORUM, AQUARIUM,
LAUDANUM AND COMPENDIUM ...

ASTERIX, THE HERO OF THESE ADVENTURES. A SHREWD, CUNNING LITTLE WARRIOR, ALL PERILOUS MISSIONS ARE IMMEDIATELY ENTRUSTED TO HIM. ASTERIX GETS HIS SUPERHUMAN STRENGTH FROM THE MAGIC POTION BREWED BY THE DRUID GETAFIX . . .

OBELIX, ASTERIX'S INSEPARABLE FRIEND. A MENHIR DELIVERY MAN BY TRADE, ADDICTED TO WILD BOAR. OBELIX IS ALWAYS READY TO DROP EVERYTHING AND GO OFF ON A NEW ADVENTURE WITH ASTERIX − SO LONG AS THERE'S WILD BOAR TO EAT AND PLENTY OF FIGHTING. HIS CONSTANT COMPANION IS DOGMATIX, THE ONLY KNOWN CANINE ECOLOGIST, WHO HOWLS WITH DESPAIR WHEN A TREE IS CUT DOWN.

GETAFIX, THE VENERABLE VILLAGE DRUID, GATHERS MISTLETOE AND BREWS MAGIC POTIONS. HIS SPECIALITY IS THE POTION WHICH GIVES THE DRINKER SUPERHUMAN STRENGTH. BUT GETAFIX ALSO HAS OTHER RECIPES UP HIS SLEEVE . . .

CACOFONIX, THE BARD. OPINION IS DIVIDED AS TO HIS MUSICAL GIFTS. CACOFONIX THINKS HE'S A GENIUS. EVERY-ONE ELSE THINKS HE'S UNSPEAKABLE. BUT SO LONG AS HE DOESN'T SPEAK, LET ALONE SING, EVERYBODY LIKES HIM . . .

FINALLY, VITALSTATISTIX, THE CHIEF OF THE TRIBE. MAJESTIC, BRAVE AND HOT-TEMPERED, THE OLD WARRIOR IS RESPECTED BY HIS MEN AND FEARED BY HIS ENEMIES. VITALSTATISTIX HIMSELF HAS ONLY ONE FEAR, HE IS AFRAID THE SKY MAY FALL ON HIS HEAD TOMORROW. BUT AS HE ALWAYS SAYS, TOMORROW NEVER COMES.

A PIRATE SHIP IS SAILING CAUTIOUSLY ALONG THE MARE BRITANNICUM, THE CHANNEL SEPARATING BRITAIN FROM THE CONTINENT...

RIGHT! WE'VE MANAGED TO SAVE UP ENOUGH TO BUY THIS BOAT, BUT WATCH OUT! STEER CLEAR OF THE GAULS!

SHIP TO PORT, CAP'N!

ARE THEY GAULS, BY TOUTATIS?

NO! ROMAN SHIP TO PORT, BY JUPITER!

HARRH! HARRH! HARRH! A GOOD PORTENT!

CAP'N... IT'S A WHOLE ROMAN FLEET TO PORT!

?!?

WHAT THE... WE MUST FLEE! AND FAST... BE FLEET ABOUT IT!

TOO LATE!

WE WEREN'T FLEET ENOUGH, CAP'N!

O FORTUNATOS NIMIUM, SUA SI BONA NORINT AGRICOLAS!

YOU MIGHT TELL ME WHAT ALL THAT WAS INSTEAD OF MAKING SILLY JOKES, YOUNG FELLER-ME-LAD!

THAT, AS IT HAPPENED, WAS JULIUS CAESAR WITH HIS ENTIRE ARMY AND NAVY, OFF TO INVADE BRITAIN.

BRITAIN HAD OFTEN HELPED GAUL FIGHT THE ROMANS, SO NOW THAT THE GAULS WERE CONQUERED JULIUS CAESAR HAD DECIDED TO TAKE SHIP AT PORTUS ITIUS (BOULOGNE) AND INVADE THE BRITISH ISLES...

HIBERNIA
CALEDONIA
BRITAIN
MAMUCIUM
GLEVUM
CAMULODUNUM
LONDINIUM
BELGARUM
DUROVERNUM
DUBRAE
PORTUS ITIUS
GAUL

THE BRITONS WERE RATHER LIKE THE GAULS MANY OF THEM BEING DESCENDED FROM GAULISH TRIBES WHO HAD SETTLED IN BRITAIN. THEY SPOKE THE SAME LANGUAGE, BUT WITH SOME PECULIAR EXPRESSIONS OF THEIR OWN...

GOODNESS GRACIOUS! THIS IS A JOLLY RUM THING, EH, WHAT?

I SAY, RATHER, OLD FRUIT!

THE BRITONS WERE LED BY THEIR CHIEF CASSIVELLAUNOS...

BUT IN SPITE OF THEIR GALLANTRY, THE BRITONS HAD SOME STRANGE CUSTOMS WHICH WERE RATHER A DRAWBACK IN BATTLE...

I SAY, OLD CHAP, I THINK IT'S GETTING ON FOR TIME!

TIME? TIME FOR WHAT?

BANG!

AWFULLY SORRY! WE'LL BE BACK LATER.

WHERE ARE THEY GOING, BY JUPITER?

NO IDEA, BY MERCURY! LETTING US DOWN LIKE THIS IN MID-FIGHT! IT'S NOT DONE!

...THEY STOPPED AT FIVE O'CLOCK EVERY DAY TO DRINK HOT WATER...

JUST A SPOT OF MILK, PLEASE!

RIGHTY-HO, LUV.

PLEASE MAY I HAVE SOME MARMALADE?

MARMALADE'S OFF!

MOREOVER, THEY STOPPED FIGHTING TWO DAYS OUT OF EVERY SEVEN...

AWFULLY SORRY! IT'S THE WEEKEND, Y'KNOW!

THIS IS REALLY GETTING ME DOWN!!!

ACCORDINGLY JULIUS CAESAR, A CUNNING STRATEGIST, DECIDED TO FIGHT ONLY AT FIVE O'CLOCK ON WEEKDAYS AND ALL DAY AT THE WEEKEND...

OH, I SAY, THE CADS!

ATTACK, BY JUNO!

SO CASSIVELLAUNOS SOON HAD TO SURRENDER. ALL BRITAIN WAS OCCUPIED...

SPQR

ALL? NO... ONE VILLAGE STILL HOLDS OUT AGAINST THE INVADERS. ONE SMALL VILLAGE IN CANTIUM...

THE SMALL VILLAGE STILL HOLDING OUT SUCCESSFULLY AGAINST THE ROMAN AGGRESSORS IS INHABITED BY A TOUGH TRIBE OF BRITONS COMMANDED BY THEIR CHIEF MYKINGDOMFORANOS...

CRACK

CHIEFTAINS FROM ALL OVER BRITAIN MEET HERE, UNITED BY THEIR LOVE OF LIBERTY, AMONG THEM HIBERNIANS AND CALEDONIANS...

OCH AYE, ANTICLIMAX! O'VEROPTIMISTIX AND MYSELF WERE BIDDEN HERE BY YON LAIRD.

I SAY, MCANIX, WE'RE IN A BIT OF A FIX, OLD BOY!

SURE ENOUGH...

WE CAN'T HOLD OUT AGAINST THE ROMANS MUCH LONGER. WE NEED HELP?

NAE SUGAR, MON, JUST A WEE DRAPPIE O' MILK.

I'VE GOT A FIRST COUSIN ONCE REMOVED LIVING IN GAUL. HIS VILLAGE HAS BEEN HOLDING OUT AGAINST THE ROMANS FOR AGES. I HEARD THEY'VE GOT A MAGIC POTION WHICH GIVES THEM SUPERHUMAN STRENGTH.

3A

ANTICLIMAX, YOU'D BETTER GO TO GAUL TO SEE YOUR COUSIN AND BRING BACK SOME OF THIS MAGIC POTION!

OH, I SAY, JOLLY GOOD SHOW! THIS IS MY CHANCE TO SEE MY DEAR COUSIN ASTERIX AGAIN. HAVEN'T SEEN HIM FOR AGES, WHAT!

TO THE SUCCESS OF YOUR MISSION!

AND AFTER DARK...

JOLLY GOOD LUCK, OLD BOY, AND ALL THAT SORT OF THING...

THE NIMBLE ANTI-CLIMAX MANAGES TO SLIP THROUGH THE ROMAN LINES...

ALL QUIET TONIGHT. THERE'S NO FOG; THE BRITONS WON'T TRY ANYTHING.

...AND REACHES THE COAST, WHERE HE SETS OFF FOR GAUL IN A LITTLE JOLLY-BOAT.

ANTICLIMAX WAS BROUGHT UP IN THE TRIBE OF THE OXBRIGIENSES, FAMED FOR THEIR SKILL IN ROWING.

SPLAT!

SPLAT!

PEACE REIGNS IN THE LITTLE GAULISH VILLAGE WE KNOW SO WELL. IN FACT IT IS REIGNING SO HARD THAT...

I'M BORED, ASTERIX! THERE ARE HARDLY ANY ROMANS LEFT AT ALL.

OBELIX, YOU KNOW PERFECTLY WELL MOST OF THE ROMANS ARE IN BRITAIN.

IT'S NOT FAIR! WHY CAN'T THE BRITONS COME HERE IF THEY WANT SOME FUN WITH ROMANS INSTEAD OF TAKING THEM OVER TO BRITAIN?

FOR THE LAST TIME, OBELIX, THE BRITONS DID NOT TAKE ANY ROMANS OVER TO...

AHEM!

SPLOSH!

I SAY, GENTLEMEN, COULD YOU TELL ME WHERE MR. ASTERIX LIVES, WHAT?

?!

I'M ASTERIX!

OH, I SAY, WHAT A BIT OF LUCK! I'M ANTI-CLIMAX. LET'S SHAKE HANDS, OLD BOY.

ANTICLIMAX! MY FIRST COUSIN ONCE REMOVED!

AND THIS IS MY BEST FRIEND OBELIX!

RIGHT!

ANY FRIEND OF ASTERIX IS A FRIEND OF MINE! SIR, I SHOULD BE VERY PROUD IF YOU WOULD SHAKE ME BY THE HAND!

OBELIX!

BOM! BOM! BOM! BOM!

BUT HE'S BEEN REMOVED ONCE ANYWAY, AND HE ASKED ME TO...

HE'S MY FIRST COUSIN ONCE REMOVED FROM BRITAIN, AND THEY DON'T TALK QUITE THE SAME AS US!

JOLLY GOOD SHOW, WHAT!

WHAT STRENGTH! I SUPPOSE YOU GET IT FROM THE MAGIC POTION, WHAT?

YES, OBELIX FELL INTO THE MAGIC POTION WHEN HE WAS A BABY...

WE'LL NEVER HEAR THE END OF THAT!

ACTUALLY, COUSIN ASTERIX, YOUR MAGIC POTION IS JUST WHAT WE NEED TO HELP US FIGHT THE ROMANS, WHAT!

COME ON, ANTICLIMAX. LET'S GO AND TALK TO OUR CHIEF VITALSTATISTIX.

WHAT DO YOU KEEP ON SAYING WHAT FOR?

I SAY, SIR, DON'T YOU KNOW WHAT'S WHAT, WHAT?

MAY I ??!

HE WAS ONCE REMOVED. BUT YOU MUSTN'T SHAKE HIM TOO HARD EVEN IF HE ASKS YOU TO.

?

ONCE ASTERIX HAS EXPLAINED MATTERS RATHER MORE CLEARLY THAN OBELIX...

WE'LL HELP YOU! I WILL ASK OUR DRUID GETAFIX TO MAKE SOME MAGIC POTION. LOTS OF MAGIC POTION!

COME AND SEE ROUND MY HOUSE AND GARDEN WHILE WE'RE WAITING, ANTICLIMAX.

A GARDEN IS A LOVESOME THING, GOD WOT!

WHAT'S WOT, WHAT?

WHAT CAN I OFFER YOU, ANTICLIMAX? A BOAR? GOAT'S MILK? BEER?

A CUP OF HOT WATER WITH A SPOT OF MILK, PLEASE.

???

I LIKE YOUR CLOTHES! SCRUNCH! SCRUNCH!

THIS MATERIAL COMES FROM CALEDONIA. IT'S CALLED TWEED.

SLURP! SLURP! DOES IT COST A LOT TO MAKE UP?

RATHER! MY TAILOR MAKES A GOOD THING OUT OF IT.

COME ALONG TO MY PLACE! THE MAGIC POTION'S READY. IT'S TO TAKE AWAY, ISN'T IT?

THIS BARREL WILL GIVE YOUR WHOLE TRIBE SUPERHUMAN STRENGTH, AND THE ROMANS A REAL HEADACHE.

I SAY, I'M MOST FRIGHTFULLY GRATEFUL, O DRUID GETAFIX!

BUT HOW AM I TO GET THIS HUGE BARREL HOME TO BRITAIN ALL BY MYSELF?

WELL, OF COURSE YOU COULD DRINK SOME OF THE POTION TO MAKE YOU STRONG ENOUGH TO CARRY IT, BUT THAT WOULD BE A WASTE OF POTION...

RATHER!

ARE YOU THINKING WHAT I'M THINKING, OBELIX?

OH, DO LET'S, ASTERIX! THE ROMANS HAVE GONE TO BRITAIN, SO LET'S GO AND HAVE SOME FUN WITH THEM IN BRITAIN!

RIGHT, ANTICLIMAX! IF OUR CHIEF SAYS YES, WE'LL GO BACK TO BRITAIN WITH YOU!

OH, JOLLY GOOD SHOW, OLD FRUIT!

LOOK, HERE COMES THE CHIEF!

ALL RIGHT, ASTERIX, I AGREE! YOU CAN MAKE A LANDING IN BRITAIN. THERE ARE SO FEW ROMANS LEFT IN THESE PARTS WE CAN DO WITHOUT YOU FOR A BIT.

OH, I SAY, WHAT A BIT OF LUCK!

WE'RE GOING TO SEE THE ROMANS! WE'RE GOING TO SEE THE ROMANS! TRALALA!

WOOF!
WOOF!

WAIT A MINUTE. I'LL GIVE YOU SOME GOURDS OF POTION FOR THE JOURNEY.

WHAT ARE THESE STRANGE HERBS, GETAFIX?

OH, THEY COME FROM VERY FAR AWAY. I HAVEN'T FOUND OUT WHAT THEY'RE FOR YET. YOU CAN TAKE SOME IF YOU LIKE.

10

OUR FRIENDS HAVE FINISHED PACKING AND SAID GOODBYE...

YOU'LL BE A GOOD LITTLE DOG WHILE I'M AWAY, WON'T YOU, DOGMATIX?

SNIFF!

AND THE WHOLE VILLAGE GATHERS TO SEE THE BRAVE TRAVELLERS OFF.

LYRE? WHAT LYRE? DEAR ME, NO, CACOFONIX, I HAVEN'T SEEN YOUR LYRE!

BUT HOW AM I TO SING MY FAREWELL SONG, THEN?

CRACK!

WE SHOULD HAVE BROUGHT SOME FOOD WITH US.

GOOD GRACIOUS ME, OLD CHAP, WHAT FOR? BRITISH FOOD'S DELICIOUS. YOU'RE SURE TO LIKE IT, WHAT!

THERE'S MY LITTLE JOLLY-BOAT.

IT'S A JOLLY LITTLE BOAT!

IT IS SMALLER THAN THE GARDEN OF MY UNCLE...

BUT IT IS LARGER THAN THE PEN OF MY AUNT.

AT THIS VERY MOMENT A ROMAN GALLEY IS LEAVING DUBRAE (DOVER) FOR GAUL, WITH PART OF THE GARRISON OF THE FORTIFIED CAMP OF AQUARIUM ON BOARD...

YOU'LL BE GLAD TO GET BACK TO YOUR QUIET FORTIFIED CAMP AT AQUARIUM AFTER YOUR TOUGH CAMPAIGN AGAINST THE BRITONS, O TULLIUS STRATOCUMULUS.

THERE'S A VILLAGE OF LUNATICS IN MY DISTRICT, AND BY JUPITER, I'D RATHER ANY SORT OF CAMPAIGN THAN RUN INTO THEM AGAIN!

LITTLE JOLLY-BOAT RIGHT AHEAD!

?!

11

THE FOG LIFTS, REVEALING A SORRY SIGHT...

MERCY! MERCY! MERCY! MERCY! MERCY! MERCY!

OOPS!

RIGHT, THEY'VE GONE. LET'S GET EVERYTHING SHIPSHAPE. AND... ER... WE WON'T MENTION IT AGAIN, WILL WE?

♫♫ ♫

OH YES, WE WILL MENTION IT AGAIN! THOSE INDOMITABLE GAULS ARE ON THEIR WAY TO BRITAIN WITH A BARREL OF MAGIC POTION! I HEARD THEM SAY SO! WE MUST WARN OUR LEADERS IN BRITAIN!

GO... GO BACK TO BRITAIN?

J...JUST FOR A LITTLE MAGIC POTION? ANYWAY, AREN'T THEY LAYING IT ON A BIT THICK ABOUT THIS POTION?

NO, CAPTAIN, THEY ARE NOT!

OH, ALL RIGHT! ALEA JACTA EST. WE'LL GO BACK TO BRITAIN.

MEANWHILE OUR FRIENDS ARE NEARING THE BRITISH COAST...

DO YOU OFTEN GET FOG LIKE THAT?

GOODNESS, NO, OLD CHAP! ONLY WHEN IT ISN'T RAINING.

SOON AFTERWARDS...

YOU KNOW WHAT, ASTERIX? I THINK A TUNNEL BETWEEN GAUL AND BRITAIN WOULD BE A GOOD IDEA. THEN PEOPLE COULD KEEP OUT OF THE RAIN AND THE FOG ON THE CROSSING.

WE'VE BEEN THINKING OF A TUNNEL OURSELVES. WE'VE EVEN STARTED DIGGING ONE, BUT IT LOOKS LIKE TAKING A JOLLY LONG TIME, WHAT!

I'LL TAKE YOU TO A FRIENDLY PUB WHERE THEY'LL GIVE YOU YOUR FIRST BRITISH MEAL.

AT LAST! I WAS GETTING REALLY HUNGRY!

I HOPE THEY'VE GOT BOAR!

CAN'T YOU SEE THE SIGN?

THE JOLLY BOAR

THAT DOESN'T MEAN A THING. I ONCE KNEW A PLACE CALLED 'THE WARM WELCOME', AND THEY...

SSH, OBELIX!

HELLO, LANDLORD!

GOODNESS ME, IT'S ANTICLIMAX!

PSSPSSPSS PSSPSSPSS

OH, I SAY!

ANTICLIMAX SAYS YOU'RE FRIENDS. PLEASED TO MEET YOU! I'M SURE YOU CAN DO WITH A GOOD MEAL...

BUT THEN YOU'LL HAVE TO LEAVE. THE ROMANS ARE KEEPING TABS ON CLOSING TIME.

THREE BEERS WHILE WE'RE WAITING, OLD CHAP!

EEAGH...

ISN'T IT WARM ENOUGH? I CAN GET THEM TO TAKE THE CHILL OFF...

RIGHT! THE BOAR'S READY!

AHA!

THIS IS A BIT OF A JOLLY OLD BORE, WHAT!

EAT UP, OBELIX, AND DON'T PASS REMARKS. IN BRITAIN YOU MUST DO AS THE BRITONS DO.

BUT BOILED, WITH MINT SAUCE, ASTERIX! POOR THING!

15

16

LONDINIUM. THE PALACE OF THE ROMAN GOVERNOR...

...IN WHOSE OFFICE THE ATMOSPHERE IS NOT EXACTLY CORDIAL.

THEY MANAGED TO GET PAST OUR PATROLS, O ENCYCLOPAEDICUS BRITANNICUS. THEY'RE MAKING FOR LONDINIUM.

THEY MUST BE CAPTURED, BY JUNO! THIS IS VITAL! I MUST HAVE THAT BARREL OF MAGIC POTION!

THEY'LL PROBABLY TAKE REFUGE IN A PUBLIC HOUSE. SEARCH THEM ALL AND CONFISCATE EVERY BARREL.

AND IF YOU DON'T FIND IT I'LL HAVE YOU BOILED AND SERVED TO THE LIONS! WITH MINT SAUCE!

HOW HORRIBLE!

YES, POOR CREATURES!

MEANWHILE, IN A LITTLE WOOD NEAR LONDINIUM...

THE CITY GATES WILL BE GUARDED... WE'D BETTER WAIT FOR THE FOG. THEN WE CAN SLIP PAST.

BUT THAT MIGHT TAKE AGES!

OH NO, OLD BOY! FOG COMES DOWN JOLLY FAST AT THIS...

...TIME OF YEAR.

THESE BRITONS ARE CRAZY!

JUST WHAT I WAS GOING TO SAY, ASTERIX!

COME ON!

SOON AFTERWARDS...

HERE WE ARE!

WAIT... THERE'S A RIOT GOING ON OVER THERE!

THAT'S NOT A RIOT. I SAY, YOU'RE IN LUCK! THAT'S A VERY POPULAR GROUP. THEY'RE TOP OF THE BARDIC CHARTS.

IF ONLY CACOFONIX COULD SEE THIS!

EEEEEE

THE JUG AND AMPHORA

GAULISH WINES OUR SPECIALITY

WE'LL FIND FRIENDS IN HERE

POM POM POM... POM POM POM POM...

OH, IT'S YOU AND THE GAULS, ANTICLIMAX. YOU CAN COME IN, THERE AREN'T ANY ROMANS ABOUT.

HELLO DIPSOMANIAX!

THE ROMANS ARE ON YOUR TRACK. YOU'D BETTER STAY HIDDEN IN LONDINIUM UNTIL THE FUSS HAS DIED DOWN. THEN YOU CAN GO ON TO THE REBEL VILLAGE LATER.

I'LL HIDE YOUR BARREL IN MY CELLAR WITH MY BARRELS OF GAULISH WINE.

SOON AFTERWARDS...

WHAT WOULD YOU LIKE TO WASH DOWN YOUR BOILED BOAR? HOT WATER, WARM BEER, ICED RED WINE...

ON THE HOUSE, OF COURSE.

BY THE WAY, WHAT SORT OF MONEY DO YOU USE HERE?

IT'S REALLY AWFULLY SIMPLE, OLD BOY...

WE HAVE IRON INGOTS WEIGHING A POUND WHICH ARE WORTH THREE AND A HALF SESTERTII EACH, AND FIVE NEW BRONZE COINS WHICH ARE WORTH TWELVE OLD BRONZE COINS. SESTERTII ARE EACH WORTH TWELVE BRONZE COINS AND...

THESE BRITONS ARE...

DRINK UP YOUR BEER BEFORE IT GETS COLD.

?!?

OPEN IN THE NAME OF CAESAR!

POM POM! POM!

THERE'S NO ONE ABOUT AT NIGHT BUT ROMAN SOLDIERS, OLD BOY! YOU CAN'T DO ANYTHING TILL TOMORROW.

WELL, WE'LL TAKE THE CHANCE TO GET A BIT OF SLEEP.

A LITTLE LATER, AFTER DARK, STRANGE ACTIVITIES MAY BE OBSERVED OUTSIDE THE GOVERNOR'S PALACE...

ALL THE BARRELS IN THE CELLARS OF THE CITY INNS HAVE BEEN CONFISCATED AND ARE NOW IN THE CELLARS OF THE PALACE, O ENCYCLOPAEDICUS BRITANNICUS!

EXCELLENT! NOW I WANT ALL THE MEN TO START TASTING THE BARRELS...

THAT WAY WE MAY BE LUCKY ENOUGH TO FIND THE BARREL OF MAGIC POTION! ACTION STATIONS!

AND IN THE PALACE CELLAR WE ARE ONCE MORE PRIVILEGED TO WATCH THAT ASTONISHING SIGHT, A ROMAN LEGION ENGAGED IN MANOEUVRES...

ON THE COMMAND! ONE BARREL PER LEGIONARY! NOTIFY YOUR COMMANDING OFFICER IF IT TASTES FUNNY! NO FALLING OUT OF LINE! ATTEN-SHUN!

CASKS... BROACH!

TCHAC!

LET'S GET OBELIX BACK TO DIPSOMANIAX'S PUB. THEN WE'LL GO AND LOOK FOR THE CART.

SOON AFTERWARDS...

THE JUG AND AMPHORA

GAULISH WINES OUR SPECIALITY

ZZZZZZ... ZZZZZZ...

WE MUST GET OUR BARREL OF POTION BACK!

OH, RATHER, WHAT!

MEANWHILE, IN THE COURTYARD OF THE GOVERNOR'S PALACE...

LEGIONARIES, I'M ASHAMED OF YOU! YOU'VE BEEN ACTING LIKE BARBARIANS, DECLINING AND FALLING ALL OVER THE PLACE! IF JULIUS CAESAR HEARS OF THIS YOU'LL BE HAVING A ROMAN HOLIDAY WITH THE LIONS IN THE CIRCUS MAXIMUS!

GET iT?

I WOULDN'T MIND BEING EATEN IF ONLY HE'D SHUT UP...

THE ONLY BARRELS THAT HAVE GONE BELONG TO DIPSOMANIAX.

RIGHT! SEARCH THAT PUB AND ARREST EVERYONE PRESENT!!!

WE'RE OFF TO LOOK FOR THE GAULS.

WE FOUND THEM.

24

30

I'M TAKING YOU TO SEE A COUSIN OF MINE. HE KEEPS A PUB TOO. HIS NAME'S SURTAX. HE MAY BE ABLE TO HELP US.

JOLLY GOOD WHEEZE, WHAT!

I SAY, COUSIN DIPSOMANIAX, I'M FEARFULLY PLEASED TO SEE YOU! I HEARD ABOUT THE ROMANS ARRESTING YOU. IT GAVE ME QUITE A TURN.

I SAY, I'M FEARFULLY PLEASED TOO, SURTAX!

WE MUSTN'T LET OUR EMOTIONS RUN AWAY WITH US. I'VE GOT SOMETHING TO SHOW YOU.

I HAD A VISITOR, WHO WAS A SHADY CHARACTER, THOUGH HE SAID HE WAS BRITISH! HE SOLD ME A BARREL WITH YOUR NAME ON IT.

?!?

DIPSOMAN

ONE OF THE STOLEN BARRELS!

I'M AFRAID IT'S NOT THE MAGIC POTION.

I HAD THE CHAP FOLLOWED. I'VE GOT HIS ADDRESS. LVII PARK LANE.

STOUT FELLER!

DIPS

IS THAT FAR?

QUITE A WAY.

YOU'D BETTER HAVE SOME BOILED BOAR BEFORE YOU START OUT.

LET'S GET AFTER THE THIEF STRAIGHT AWAY!

SOME TIME LATER...

HERE WE ARE...

NOW... No. LVII...

IT'S A GOOD JOB WE'VE GOT THE NUMBER! WE MIGHT NOT HAVE BEEN ABLE TO TELL THE HUT JUST FROM ITS DESCRIPTION.

28

WE'RE GOING TO VISIT ALL THE PUBS ON THIS LIST... THE LANDLORDS HAVE ALL BOUGHT STOLEN BARRELS, AND ONE OF THEM HAS GOT THE MAGIC POTION!

SOON AFTERWARDS...

WHAT'LL IT BE, GENTLEMEN?

DID YOU BUY ANY BARRELS OF WINE MARKED WITH THE NAME DIPSOMANIAX?

YES, ONE, THE ROMANS HAVE CONFISCATED ALL MY OTHER BARRELS. WHAT CAN I GET YOU?

A CUP OF WINE, PLEASE.

ONE CUP BETWEEN THE THREE OF YOU? YOU MUST BE CALEDONIANS, * WHAT!

* SCOTS

THAT'S WINE ALL RIGHT.

SNIFF! SNIFF! SNIFF!

SNIFF! SNIFF! SNIFF!

GOODNESS GRACIOUS! OF COURSE IT'S WINE! IT'S PERFECTLY SAFE TO DRINK IT!

NO, THANK YOU! WE WERE JUST LOOKING.

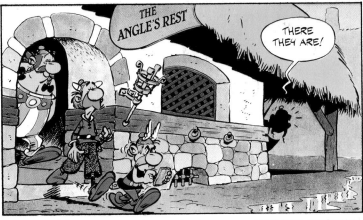

THE ANGLE'S REST

THERE THEY ARE!

SHALL WE NAB THEM?

NO. I WANT TO FIND OUT WHAT THEY WERE DOING IN THAT PUB!

THEY WANTED TO LOOK AT MY WINE. FUNNY WAYS YOU'VE GOT ON THE CONTINENT!

VERY FUNNY...

I'VE GOT IT, BY JUPITER! THOSE GAULS HAVE MISLAID THEIR BARREL AND THEY'RE LOOKING FOR IT! WE'VE ONLY GOT TO FOLLOW THEM AND THEY'LL LEAD US TO THE MAGIC POTION!

THE DOG AND DUX

WE'VE VISITED NEARLY ALL THE PUBS ON OUR LIST. NOTHING SO FAR... LET'S JUST TRY HERE.

I'VE NEVER SET EYES ON SO MUCH WINE BEFORE. DRINKING ONLY WITH MINE EYES IS ALL VERY WELL, BUT IT DOES GET A BIT TEDIOUS!

YES, I DID BUY A BARREL OF GAULISH WINE, BUT I SOLD IT TO THE CAMULODUNUM TEAM. THEY'RE PLAYING DUROVERNUM TOMORROW, YOU KNOW, WHAT!

WHAT'S HE ON ABOUT?

OH, IT'S A GAME. WE'RE MAD ON IT IN BRITAIN! YOU PLAY IT WITH A BLADDER AND XXX BRITONS DIVIDED INTO II TEAMS OF XV.

THERE'S A MATCH FOR THE TRIBAL CROWN NEAR LONDINIUM TOMORROW.

I'M JOLLY PROUD TO HAVE SOLD MY BARREL TO THE CAMULODUNUM TEAM... UP CAMULODUNUM!!!

I HOPE IT'S GOOD WINE AND IT HELPS THEM TO WIN, WHAT!

IF IT'S THE BARREL I THINK IT IS, THEY JUST CAN'T LOSE!

NEXT DAY OUR FRIENDS SET OFF FOR THE GROUND WHERE THE MATCH BETWEEN CAMULODUNUM AND DUROVERNUM IS TO TAKE PLACE...

WHAT A CROWD!

YES, IT'S QUITE A POPULAR GAME OLD BOY, RATHER!

WHAT WORRIES ME IS THAT THE ROMANS AREN'T BOTHERING US.

PERHAPS THEY'VE HAD ENOUGH OF BEING KNOCKED ABOUT. THERE ARE PLENTY LIKE THAT. YOU KNOCK THEM ABOUT AND THEN THEY'VE HAD ENOUGH.

BUT THE ROMANS ARE NOT FAR AWAY!

RIGHT! GOT IT, BY MERCURY? MINGLE WITH THE CROWD AND KEEP YOUR EYES OPEN!

THE DECURION SAID IN MUFTI, IDIOT!

WELL, I AM IN MUFTI, AREN'T I?

32

WE WANT TO SEE THE CAMULODUNUM TEAM.

YOU GO AND BUY YOUR TICKETS LIKE EVERYONE ELSE, MY FRIEND. THEN YOU CAN SEE BOTH TEAMS!

PLAYERS' ENTRANCE NO ADMITTANCE

ANYONE FOR MINT SAUCE?

NICE WARM BEER!

HOT WATER! HOT WATER!

GET YOUR TEAM'S COLOURS HERE!

?!?

STAND SEATS
TICKETS

HERE ARE OUR SEATS, OLD BOY!

WILL YOU EXPLAIN THE RULES OF THE GAME, ANTICLIMAX?

IT'S REALLY FRIGHTFULLY SIMPLE. YOU CAN DO ALMOST ANYTHING TO CARRY THE BLADDER OVER THE OTHER TEAM'S GOAL LINE. ANYTHING'S ALLOWED EXCEPT USING WEAPONS WITHOUT PREVIOUS AGREEMENT...

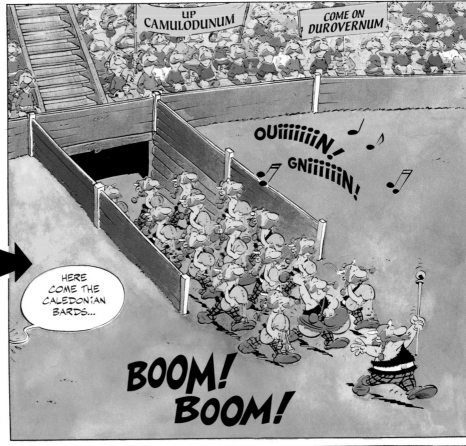

UP CAMULODUNUM

COME ON DUROVERNUM

OUiiiiiiiN! GNiiiiiiiN!

HERE COME THE CALEDONIAN BARDS...

BOOM! BOOM!

HERE'S CAMULODUNUM'S SACRED GOOSE...

UP CAMULODUNUM!

...AND DUROVERNUM'S HEN...

COME ON DUROVERNUM!

33

AND HERE COME THE PLAYERS!!!

COME ON CAMULODUNUM!

UP DUROVERNUM!

PARP

THAT'S THE DRUIDICAL REFEREE BLOWING HIS HORN FOR THE KICK-OFF...

WHAM!

34 A

DUROVERNUM OR THE TRIBAL CROWN

BOING! BOING! BOING! BOING!

WE MUST TAKE THIS NICE GAME BACK TO GAUL!

YES, BUT CAMULODUNUM DOESN'T SEEM TO BE ON TOP... AND IF THE PLAYERS HAD DRUNK THE MAGIC POTION...

PARP!

?!?

BOING! BOING! BOING!

NO... HE'S NOT PUTTING IT ON... STRETCHERS!

34 B

DUROVERNUM OR THE TRIBAL CROWN

BIFF!

I SAY, OLD CHAP, WAS THAT YOU STAMPING ON MY FACE, EH, WHAT?

LET'S NOT GET WORKED UP, OLD BOY! IT'S ONLY A GAME, AND ALL THAT SORT OF THING!

BOING!

CLAP! CLAP! CLAP!

HIPIPHURRAX HAS SCORED A TRY. NOW HE'S GOING TO TRY TO CONVERT IT.

CLAP! CLAP! CLAP! CLAP! CLAP! CLAP!

ZOOMPH!

SCORE

CAMVLODVNVM VERSVS DVROVERNVM

VIIII   III

X

THAT'S THE MAGIC POTION ALL RIGHT. COME ON!

SHIVER ME TIMBERS, BOY! WHAT BRINGS YOU DOWN FROM THE CROW'S NEST, EH?

THIS BLADDER, CAP'N! OH MY STARS!

43

YOU'VE LOST THE MAGIC POTION? THEN WE'RE DONE FOR! WHEN THE ROMANS HEAR ABOUT IT THEY'LL ATTACK, WHAT!

DINNA FASH, WE'LL DIE WI' OOR BOOTS ON!

SURE AND BEGORRAH WE WILL!

WE'RE NOT BEATEN YET, BY TOUTATIS! I'VE FOUND SOME HERBS I BROUGHT FROM HOME IN MY POCKET. WE CAN USE THEM TO MAKE THE MAGIC POTION!

BRING ME A CAULDRON OF HOT WATER! I'M GOING TO PREPARE THE MAGIC POTION!

?

I SAY, WE'RE SAVED! VERY DECENT OF YOU!

RATHER!

JOLLY GOOD SHOW!

DO YOU KNOW HOW TO MAKE THE MAGIC POTION, ASTERIX?

NO, OBELIX. ONLY OUR DRUID GETAFIX KNOWS THE SECRET OF THE MAGIC POTION...

WHEN WE LEFT OUR VILLAGE GETAFIX GAVE ME THESE HERBS. THEY MAY HAVE QUALITIES WE DON'T KNOW ABOUT. ANYWAY THEY'LL ENCOURAGE OUR BRITISH FRIENDS.

41 A

HERE'S THE HOT WATER!

I SAY, I'M MOST FRIGHTFULLY GLAD YOU CAN MAKE THE MAGIC POTION, DON'T YOU KNOW!

WILL IT TAKE LONG?

IT'S READY.

WHY, IT'S AS SIMPLE AS OUR OWN BRITISH RECIPES! I'LL CALL MY WARRIORS.

I DON'T TRUST THIS FANCY GAULISH COOKING.

THERE ISN'T ANY GARLIC IN THIS MAGIC POTION, IS THERE?

I SAY, CAN I HAVE A SPOT OF MILK WITH MY MAGIC POTION?

THESE BRITONS ARE CRAZY!

TOC! TOC! TOC! TOC! TOC!

AND NOW TO SIT BACK AND WAIT FOR THE ROMANS TO ATTACK!

41 B

BUT IF ASTERIX'S TRICK HAS INSPIRED THE BRITONS WITH FRESH COURAGE, SOME GOOD NEWS HAS RAISED THE ROMANS' MORALE TOO.

AVE, GENERAL. GOVERNOR ENCYCLO-PAEDICUS BRITANNICUS HAS SENT ME TO TELL YOU THAT THE MAGIC POTION IS AT THE BOTTOM OF THE RIVER, TOGETHER WITH ITS GAULISH ESCORT!

THIS IS THE MOMENT TO ATTACK, BY JUPITER!!! **FALL IN!** SOUND THE TRUMPETS AND BUCINAS!!!

TANTANTARA TARAAAA

AND YET AGAIN WE ARE PRIVILEGED TO VIEW THE FANTASTIC SIGHT OF A ROMAN LEGION ENGAGED IN MANOEUVRES...

CENTURIONS, DECURIONS AND OTHER RANKS! THE ENEMY HAVE LOST THEIR MAGIC POTION AND THEIR GAULISH ALLIES AT ONE FELL SWOOP! IT'S PERFECTLY SAFE NOW!

...IN SQUARE FORMATION...

THEN IMITATE THE ACTION OF THE TIBER! ON, ON, YOU NOBLEST ROMANS!

...IN TRIANGULAR FORMATION...

ATTACK!

LEGIONARIES! THIS IS TO LET YOU KNOW WE'RE HERE, AND SO IS THE MAGIC POTION! THERE'S STILL TIME TO SURRENDER!

...AND IN CIRCULAR FORMATION...

I KNOW HIM! I WAS STATIONED AT AQUARIUM. THAT'S ASTERIX, THAT IS!

AND IF ASTERIX IS THERE HIS FRIEND OBELIX CAN'T BE FAR AWAY!

WHICH OBELIX? NOT THE MAD ONE!!!

AND THEY'VE GIVEN THE BRITONS SOME MAGIC POTION!

WHEN YOU'VE QUITE FINISHED... **ATTACK!!!**

COME ON THEN, **ATTACK!** DO AS THE MAN SAYS!

BONG! BONG! BONG!

WHAT'S HAPPENED TO YOUR DISCIPLINE, BY TOUTATIS! **KINDLY ATTACK!**

SHALL WE GO, ASTERIX?

LET'S GO, MYKINGDOM-FORANOS!

THE FINAL PHASE OF THE MAGNIFICENT ROMAN MANOEUVRE... A RETREAT IN DISORDER.

GET OUT IF YOU CAN!

CRAAAASH!!!

I DON'T KNOW IF I CAN, BUT I'M GOING TO HAVE A BASH!

I'M SO KEEN TO GET BACK TO GAUL I SUGGEST WE DON'T STOP EVEN IF WE MEET THE PIRATES.

I'M IN A HURRY TOO... BUT DON'T YOU THINK IT MIGHT HURT THEIR FEELINGS?

LITTLE JOLLY-BOAT TO STARBOARD, CAP'N!

THIS IS A BRAND NEW SHIP. I DON'T WANT TO BE RECKLESS. LET'S SEE WHO'S ON BOARD THIS LITTLE BOAT...

NO!! IT'S THEM AGAIN! LET'S GET OUT OF HERE! FULL SPEED AHEAD!

AND LATER...

I'M HAPPY! SO HAPPY! I'VE DIDDLED THEM THIS TIME! I WAS FASTER THAN THEM! THEY DIDN'T SINK ME!

CRUNNNCH!

I MAY HAVE RUN AGROUND, BUT THEY DIDN'T SINK ME!

AND YOU DIDN'T WANT TO BE WRECKLESS EITHER.

FLUCTUAT NEC MERGITUR.

44A

OUR CONQUERING HEROES ARE WELCOMED HOME BY THEIR VILLAGE. A GREAT BANQUET IS ORGANISED TO CELEBRATE THEIR RETURN. ASTERIX HAS TOLD THE TALE OF HIS VISIT TO BRITAIN, AND OBELIX HAS BEEN REUNITED WITH TWO DEAR OLD FRIENDS...

MY LITTLE DOGMATIX AND ROAST BOAR! UP GAUL!

THOSE HERBS I PICKED UP AT YOUR HOUSE BEFORE I LEFT, GETAFIX... WHAT WERE THEY?

OH, THEY'RE A PLANT THAT COMES FROM FAR-OFF BARBARIAN LANDS...

AND WHAT'S IT CALLED?

TEA!

CLUNK!

44B

THE END

UDERZO & GOSCINNY